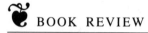 BOOK REVIEW

The diminutive format suits the
story's warm, cozy feeling, and
McPhail's watercolors feature an
endearing Emma and a poppa bear
who invites snuggling.
from THE BOOKLIST

Emma's Pet

WEEKLY READER CHILDREN'S BOOK CLUB presents

Emma's Pet

by David McPhail

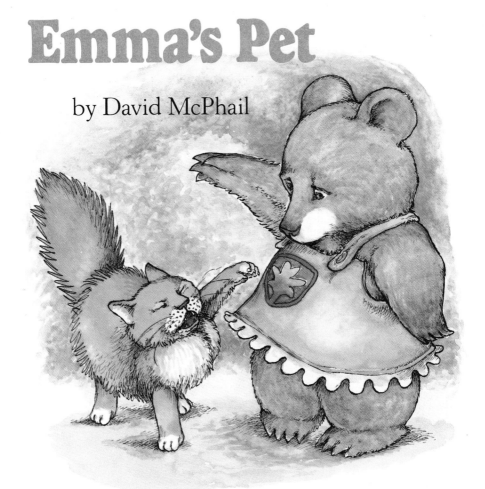

E. P. Dutton   New York

for Ashly Lee LaBrie

This book is a presentation of Weekly Reader Books.
Weekly Reader Books offers book clubs for children
from preschool through high school. For further
information write to: **Weekly Reader Books,**
4343 Equity Drive, Columbus, Ohio 43228.

Published by arrangement with E.P. Dutton.
Weekly Reader is a trademark of Field Publications.
Printed in the United States of America.

Library of Congress Cataloging in Publication Data

McPhail, David M.
    Emma's pet.
    Summary: Emma's search for a soft, cuddly pet has a
surprising ending.
    1. Children's stories, American. [1. Pets—Fiction]
I. Title.
PZ7.M2427Em 1985 [E] 85-4414
ISBN 0-525-44210-3

Editor: Ann Durell
Original edition designed by Isabel Warren-Lynch.

"I want a pet," Emma told her mother one day.
"You have a pet," said her mother.

"Fluffy's not cuddly," said Emma.
"I want a big soft cuddly pet."

So Emma went looking for a pet.

The first thing she found was a bug.
Even Emma couldn't say that was cuddly.

The mouse she found was soft and cuddly,
but it wasn't big.

The bird had nice soft feathers...

but it was too busy

feeding its family to be anybody's pet.

The frog wasn't soft and cuddly,
but it might have made a good pet…

if it hadn't taken a bath with Emma's mother.

The snake she picked up was *too* cuddly for Emma.

Then she got a fish…

but that was too wet and slippery.

And the dog she brought home
already belonged to someone else.

Emma was sad.

She sat down on a rock and began to cry.

The rock moved.
It was a turtle!

But it wasn't any softer or any more cuddly than a rock.

And then Emma saw the biggest, softest,
cuddliest thing she had ever seen.

It was her father!

"Will you be my pet?" she asked.

"Always," said her father. "Will you be mine?"
"Yes," said Emma.

And she hugged her new big soft cuddly pet.
And it hugged her right back.